Tales of the Riverbank

Hammy's New Home and other stories

DAVE ELLISON

Illustrated by
PAULINE HAZELWOOD

Scholastic Children's Books,
Scholastic Publications Ltd,
7-9 Pratt Street, London NW1 0AE

Scholastic Inc.,
730 Broadway, New York, NY 10003, USA

Scholastic Canada Ltd,
123 Newkirk Road, Richmond Hill,
Ontario, Canada L4C 3G5

Ashton Scholastic Pty Ltd,
P O Box 579, Gosford, New South Wales,
Australia

Ashton Scholastic Ltd,
Private Bag 1, Penrose, Auckland,
New Zealand

First published by Scholastic Publications Limited, 1993

Text copyright © by Dave Ellison, 1993
Illustration copyright ©by Pauline Hazelwood, 1993
Based on the TV series created by Dave Ellison and Paul Sutherland

ISBN 0 590 55250 3
Printed in Belgium by Proost Book Production

CONTENTS

HAMMY'S NEW HOME

ALL was quiet along the River Bank as the sun slowly peeped above the edges of the meadow and sent a golden shaft of light scurrying across the dew-damp grass to the water's edge. It was dawn, the beginning of a new day.

Hammy the hamster, who lived in a small burrow not far from the river, was still in bed dreaming dreams that only hamsters can dream. Without a sound, the sun's rays slipped across his face. His whiskers twitched, his nose sniffed. Gingerly he opened one eye, then the other. He twitched his whiskers again and yawned. It was time to get up. Pushing back his bedclothes he slowly found the floor with his toes, stood up and was wide awake.

Now Hammy had lived in his burrow nearly all his life. It was small, it was dark, and it was very, very dusty. No matter how often he cleaned it up, it was always dusty; and today he just didn't feel like dusting.

"No, that's it," he said to himself. "No more dusting… I'm going to move. I'll find myself a new, clean home."

Without even waiting to have breakfast, the hamster opened his front door and his search began.

"Good morning, Hammy," said a voice that seemed to come from a nearby bush.

"Oh, good morning, Mr Bush," replied the hamster.

"My name's not Bush," said the voice. "It's Rabbit - Mr Rabbit. I'm a rabbit."

Two long brown ears and a chubby round face appeared from behind the bush and Hammy saw that this was, indeed, a rabbit.

"You're out early today," said Mr Rabbit.

"Yes," replied Hammy. "I'm house hunting. You don't know where I can find an empty house, do you?"

" 'Fraid not," replied the rabbit. "My family is getting so big I have trouble finding enough homes for them…" Then, with a quick, "Cheerio…" he ran off.

Hammy wasn't too sure which way he should go to find his new home, and it was whilst he was deciding

whether to go this way or that way, that he heard a loud
"Hurrumph…Hurrumph…" followed by a thump and then another
thump and three more "Hurrumphs". Suddenly, in front of the hamster a
frog appeared, out for his morning jump.

"Oh, good morning, Mr Frog," said Hammy.

"Hurrumph," replied the frog. "You're out early today… you off
shopping or something?"

" I'm not shopping," replied the hamster. "I'm house hunting. You don't
know where I can find an empty house, do you?"

"Well," answered the frog, "there are lots of empty lily pads next to
mine, you know. We could be neighbours." Then, with a loud
"Hurrumph," he jumped away.

Now it so happened that not far from Mr Frog's lily pad home was the
home of Roderick Rat. It was a very smart riverside
residence with a large window overlooking the front

garden and a very grand oak door opening directly onto a jetty and Roderick's motor boat. Boating and anything to do with the river was the rat's favourite occupation and this morning he was getting ready for an outing. Just as he was about to start the engine, he heard someone coming along the path.

"Oh…Roderick…Roderick, wait for me…" It was Hammy, and he had arrived just in time.

"Good morning, Hammy," called Roderick. "Come on, hurry up! Jump aboard!"

The hamster ran along the jetty, climbed into the boat, and they were away.

"You're up and about nice and early," said Roderick.

"Yes," replied the hamster. "I'm house hunting. You don't know where I can find an empty house, do you?"

Roderick replied that he didn't, but perhaps their friend Mr Guinea Pig would know of one.

"We'll go and visit him," said the rat. "He knows about everything."

The guinea pig lived in an old water mill down by the big bend in the river. He was an inventor. He had invented things like the aeroplane, the hovercraft, the bath plug and the balloon. But today he hadn't invented anything, and he was beginning to wonder if any ideas would ever come to his great brain again. "Now, let's see…" he muttered to himself. " What can I think of today…?"

And it was at that moment that Hammy and Roderick arrived with the very answer.

"GP," called the rat as he came through the front door, "can you think of a place for Hammy to live? He needs a new home."

"A new home, indeed?" said GP. And then, looking at Hammy he said, "Well, it's got to be cosy, I suppose?"

"Oh, yes, please," replied Hammy.

"And dry?" the guinea pig queried.

"Oh, that would be lovely," said the hamster.

"And quiet?" continued GP.

"Oh my, oh my, yes. That's exactly what I'm looking for," sighed Hammy. "Do you know of a place just like that?"

"No," said the guinea pig. "I haven't the faintest idea." But, when he saw how disappointed Hammy looked, he gave a little chuckle and said, "I'm only joking… My great brain has just had a brilliant idea." He went on, "I know just the place for you… Come on, I'll take you there in my balloon."

Gently and in complete silence the huge balloon lifted from the ground and slowly showed itself above the tops of the trees. Swaying from side to side beneath the balloon hung a wicker basket carrying our three friends. They were off and away to find Hammy a new home.

Silently they floated across the sky. Over the wise old frog's lily pad pool, over the tall reeds and the weeping willow trees.

"Oh my, oh my, " said Hammy. "I can't wait to see my new house."

"Well, there it is," called GP, as he pointed down to an object hiding itself in the shade of a small bush. "Down we go…"

With great skill the guinea pig guided the balloon to the ground and landed with a gentle bump. In no time at all, Hammy, Roderick and Mr GP climbed out of the basket and stared at the strange object.

"Well, what do you think?" asked the guinea pig.

"Mmmm, well… I don't know," said the hamster. "It's not quite what I had in mind."

"I should think not," added the rat. "Who on earth would want to live in an old boot?"

And that's exactly what it was. Now GP had brought with him a large bag of tools, and it wasn't long before all three animals were hard at work sawing, hammering and pulling and pushing at every part of the old boot. Then, just before tea time, their work was finished. They had turned the old boot into a home. It had a front door by the heel, a downstairs window in the toe, and a bedroom window in the ankle. On top was a thatched roof and a fine stone chimney. It was cosy, it was dry and it was quiet.

"Oh, Mr Guinea Pig, it's exactly what I wanted," said the hamster.

And then he invited his friends in for tea to end the first of many happy days that Hammy would have in his old boot house.

DISCOVERY

Dark clouds scudded across the moon's face as the winter storm blew its way along the riverbank. It was cold and wet. It was the kind of night to stay at home and read a good book. Which is just what Hammy had decided to do. Curled up in front of his log fire, he was reading aloud from an old well-worn book to his friends Roderick and Mr GP.

"…And so the fine ship *September Weed* set sail. For the first few days all went well, and the passengers settled down to life at sea."

Hammy was telling the story of how the animals arrived along the riverbank many years ago. "But on the third week," he went on, "the ship was overtaken by a great storm. All the passengers were drenched as the waves tumbled over the side of the ship and the wind tore through the rigging and ripped the sails apart - "

"All those aboard the *September Weed* were cold and very frightened. The great ship drifted out of control and just as all seemed lost, the lookout, high in the mast, shouted, 'Land ahoy… Land! I can see land!' And the passengers were relieved to see that the ship was drifting towards the mouth of a small river. As they scurried around getting all their possessions together ready to go ashore, there was a loud crunch and the *September Weed* shuddered to a halt. The ship had hit a rock. All the animals scrambled ashore, but most of their possessions were lost as the great ship sank to the bottom of the river. The poor wet and bedraggled passengers were left to become the first settlers along the Riverbank."

"Well, that's some story," said the guinea pig.

"I wonder if the wreck is still there," asked the hamster.

"No, I shouldn't think so," said the rat. "After all, that was a very long time ago."

"We could always go and look," said GP.

"What, under all that water?" said Hammy. "We'd get wet."

"No, you wouldn't," answered the guinea pig. "We could use my diving bell."

Now the diving bell was one of Mr GP's great inventions. It was a splendid machine specially designed to make journeys to the bottom of the sea. But to those who didn't know, it could quite easily be mistaken for an old school bell. However, the guinea pig said it was a diving bell, and he should know. It had a large porthole, a small hatch, a headlamp, an anchor,

lots of chain and a hook; and Guinea Pig kept it in a shed behind his old mill.

Next morning, when the storm had blown itself away, the three friends could be seen preparing the wonderful machine, dragging it down to the water's edge and making it ready for the great adventure. There was, however, one slight problem. Who was going to take the bell down?

"I'm much too big," said GP. "I'd never get through the hatch."

"My tail's too long," said Roderick. "I'd get it tangled up with all the controls."

So it was left to Hammy to volunteer.

A strong rope was attached to the bell's handle, taken up to the branch of a tree overhanging the river and back down to the riverbank. Hammy climbed aboard, GP closed the hatch, and Roderick gave the order to haul away.

GP and the rat pulled on the rope. The bell swung out to the middle of the river and Hammy's dive began. Down, down he went. With gurgles and plops, splashes and sploshes, the great bell made its way to the bottom. Hammy skilfully turned the wheel, pulled the levers and guided the bell through the weeds. But he couldn't find the wreck, and he was just about to give up when a fish swam in front of the porthole.

"Good morning," he bubbled.

"Oh!…Good morning," replied Hammy, just a little bit surprised to find himself talking to a fish.

"What brings you down here?" asked the fish.

The hamster explained about the wreck and asked if he knew where it might be.

"Follow me," gurgled the fish. "I know just where it is."

And away he swam. Hammy moved the controls and the bell followed close behind. Past the swaying weeds they went. Past the sunken log, past the long roots of Mr Frog's lily pad home, and then they were there. The fish looked through the porthole and pointed down with one of his fins.

"There," he bubbled. "That's all that's left." And he swam away.

Hammy looked down and saw beneath him an old anchor, a long rusty cannon and then, half hidden under a clump of weeds, something that looked like a box with handles on the side.

"Well," said the hamster to himself, "that looks the easiest thing to take up."

And with that, he pulled a lever, lowered the bell's hook and caught hold of the handle. Then with a turn of the controls, he took the bell back to the surface.

"It's a chest!" shouted Roderick. "Quick, let's open it."

"Oh, Roderick," said Hammy. "Is it a treasure chest?"

The three friends pushed and pulled at the catch on the lid and, just before the afternoon made way for evening, there was a loud *click!* The catch flew apart, and the chest was open.

The three friends peeked inside and couldn't believe what they saw.

"Oh my, oh my," said the hamster. "What have we found?"

"It's gold," said Roderick.

"It's diamonds," said Guinea Pig.

"It's treasure," said Hammy.

And indeed it was.

THE PICNIC

It was a warm summer's day, and everyone along the riverbank was busy. The bees were busy buzzing, the birds were busy tweeting and the fish were busy bubbling. The river itself was busy gurgling and rippling along its whole length, and Roderick, as always, was busy polishing his boat.

"Just one more rub there, and a little bit there… and it's finished. Now what shall I do?" he said to no-one in particular. "I could do the gardening, or I could do the housework." But he didn't like either of these ideas, so he thought a bit more.

"I know," he said to himself, "I'll visit Hammy."

With that, he jumped into his boat, and set off.

Now, Hammy wasn't busy. He had been busy, but now he was bored. Very bored.

Then, just as he thought he was as bored as he could possibly get, he heard a motor boat coming along the river. It was Roderick.

"Hello, Hammy!" called the rat. "You don't look very busy today."

The hamster ran down to the river's edge to meet his friend and said, "No, Roderick, I'm not busy. I'm bored."

"Oh, well, we'll soon change that," replied Roderick. "Let's go for a picnic."

Now, Roderick hadn't come prepared for a picnic, though he had brought his shopping basket. So they decided to call in at the general store to buy some cakes and fruit from Miss Much.

Miss Much ran the only shop along the riverbank and she was always busy. Busy serving her customers, busy filling up her shelves, and busy counting her money. Miss Much had everything in her shop. Things like ice cream, paint and tea and long lengths of rope; oranges and apples, screws and sausages and boxes of nails. Miss Much stocked everything.

It was just as well she did. Because when Roderick and Hammy arrived, it

seemed that they wanted to buy everything.

They bought oranges and grapes, a large loaf of bread, cakes and biscuits, a pot of honey and a bunch of carrots. Then, just as the basket was almost filled to the brim, Hammy said, "Oh, yes, I almost forgot. Can we have a bottle of lemonade?"

Meanwhile, Mr Guinea Pig was very busy, too. He was busy working on his balloon.

"There's no doubt about it," he muttered. "Ballooning is by far the best way to get along the riverbank."

He was just congratulating himself on inventing such a wonderful machine, when Roderick and Hammy came round the river bend in the motor boat.

"Hello, GP," called Roderick. "We're going for a picnic. Do you want to come with us?"

"Oh, yes, please," replied the guinea pig. "I've been so busy all day I forgot to have my lunch." But there was one problem. Roderick, Hammy, the shopping basket and all the food completely filled the boat. No matter how hard he tried, GP just couldn't fit on board. "Well," he said. "We'll have to go in my balloon." Which is exactly what they did.

With the three friends, the shopping basket and all the food safely loaded on board, Guinea Pig untied a rope and the great balloon lifted slowly into the sky.

Now, not everyone was busy doing something - some people were busy doing nothing. Mr Turtle was busy sleeping. But, just as he was about to give a loud snore, something fell out of the sky and landed with a splosh right on top of his shell.

"Oh, bless my soul…it's raining apples!" he said as he opened one eye, turned his head, and looked at his back.

"Sorry!" called a voice from the sky. "It fell out of the basket…"

"Humph!" grumbled the turtle. "Raining apples, talking sky - what *is* the world coming to?" Without waiting for an answer, he went back to sleep. And the balloon went on with its journey.

"Oh, look," called Hammy as he pointed down to the ground. "That's Mr Hedgehog - he looks very busy." And he was. He was out looking for something to eat.

"Yoo-hoo…!" called Hammy.

"Mr Hedgehog, we're up here…"

"Good grief!" said the hedgehog. "You gave me a fright!"

Then, just as he was about to ask if they could see anything for him to eat from up there, a loud thump came from just in front of him, and he was looking at a large, juicy apple. Just what he had been searching for!

22

"Guinea Pig," shouted the rat, "if you don't control this balloon more carefully, all our apples will have fallen out…"

At about this time, the wise old frog was particularly busy. He was particularly busy sitting on his lily pad and as he sat on his lily pad being particularly busy, he heard three loud plops and there, right in front of him, half submerged in the water, were what looked like three more frogs, sound asleep.

"There's Mr Frog," said Hammy, as he peered over the side of the basket.

"Yes, and there go three more apples," replied Roderick. "Can't you steer this thing any better?" But it was no use. Guinea Pig wasn't listening. He was busy taking the great balloon down to skim over the lily pads.

"Afternoon, Mr Frog," called GP, as they whooshed over the top of the frog's head.

"Good afternoon," replied Mr Frog, "…three friends have just dropped in…" But by that time, GP, Roderick and Hammy were far away.

"I'm feeling hungry," said the hamster.

"Yes, I'm feeling a bit peckish," said Roderick and then went on, "Don't you think it's time we got back to the ground, GP?"

"Hold tight, then," replied the guinea pig. "Going down…" And with that, he pulled on a rope and the balloon made its way gently down to land.

"There," said the guinea pig. "Just the place for a picnic."

"What do you mean?" grumbled Roderick. "Look where we've landed!"

"Oh," said GP. "We seem to be back at my old mill." And that's exactly where they were. They had been busy all afternoon, flying round in a great big circle. But the hamster wasn't listening to any of this. He was much too busy enjoying his picnic.

Say Cheese!

It was night, and all along the riverbank was still. An owl called its eerie call as it swooped low across the surface of the water and was gone. A distant nightjar sang its lonely song. All was well - except for one thing. A strange glow of light was coming from behind the wild wood.

"It seems to be coming from GP's old mill," said Roderick. "Perhaps we should go and see if he is all right."

"That's a good idea," replied Hammy. "I'll go and get a torch."

The path they took ran along the river's edge, past the tall reeds and thick tufts of bracken and past the wild wood. Both animals kept close to each other as they gingerly made their way towards the mysterious light.

"Goodness me!" cried Roderick, as they arrived within sight of the mill. "There's light coming from every window, door and crack in the building." And then, after a moment's pause, he went on, "It looks just as though it's haunted."

"Ghosts…" trembled Hammy. "Oh my, I'm off."

"Hey! Wait for me," shouted the rat. And they were gone.

"Well, well," said Miss Much to herself next morning as she opened the door of her shop. "Who put *that* on the notice board?"

There, covering nearly all of the board, was a sign which read,

Now, Miss Much had always wanted to have a picture of herself, so she decided then and there to visit the famous Mr GP that very morning. So also did Mr Rabbit, who found GP's notice tied to a large cabbage in his vegetable garden.

"I could give a copy of the portrait to all my grandchildren," he said.

And so it went on. Animals from one end of the river to the other saw the notice and decided to have a portrait done by the famous GP.

Much later that afternoon, Hammy and Roderick cautiously made their way along the river, back to GP's house.

"It looks safe enough," said Roderick as he tied the boat to a post near the Old Mill. "Come on, let's take a look through the door."

The two friends made their way slowly forward.

"Go on, Hammy," whispered the rat. "Open the door."

With a creak and a groan and quite a few squeaks, the heavy door swung open. There standing in front of them was Guinea Pig.

"Hello, you two," he said. "Have you come to have your portrait taken?"

"Er, no…" replied a rather startled Roderick. "We've come to save you from the ghostly lights!"

"Ghostly lights? What ghostly lights?" asked GP. "The only lights I've got are in my studio…I'm a photographer. I take portraits with my camera."

"Camera? What's a camera?" asked the hamster.

"Why, it's my latest invention," replied GP. "Look, here it is."

And with that the guinea pig turned on a switch and the inside of the mill was filled with light that came from six large lamps hanging from the beams. There, in the middle of the room, standing on three thin wooden legs, was a strange object.

"Looks like a box to me," said Roderick.

"Yes," said Hammy. "A box hiding under a black sheet."

"Well, that's where you're wrong," said Guinea Pig. "That's my camera and these are my lights." And then he went on to say, "I've been up all night getting the lights to shine as bright as day, and all morning I've been taking portraits. Come on, I'll take your portraits and I'll show you how it's done."

Without waiting for a reply, the guinea pig pushed his two friends in front of the camera, put his head under the black sheet, and said, "Say *cheese*." Then he pushed a button on the camera and with a loud *click!* it was done.

"That's it… Got it…" said the excited guinea pig. "I've taken your portrait."

"Oh my," said Hammy. "I didn't feel a thing."

"And I don't even like cheese," said Roderick.

"I've got to go into a dark room now to make the negative," said GP.

And then, pointing to a pile of glass plates on the studio floor, he went on to say, "If you want to help, you can collect all those negatives I took this morning and put them in that box." And off he went.

"Oh my," said Hammy. "I've never collected negatives before in all my life."

"Oh, it's easy," said Roderick, as he started to carry some across to Hammy. "Here, we'll put them - ooh…aahhaa…" *Crash!* Roderick had tripped over one of the camera's legs and all the negatives smashed to the ground.

"Oh my," said Hammy. "I think we've broken the negatives." Which, unfortunately, was true. Now, not wanting to disappoint GP, Roderick and Hammy decided to glue the negatives together, and they had just finished their sticky task when Guinea Pig came out of the darkroom.

"Well, I've made your negative," he said. "Now we can make your picture."

But printing the picture didn't work out in quite the way that the guinea pig had intended.

"I didn't know that Miss Much had frog's legs," said Roderick, as he looked at the first print to be made.

"She hasn't," said GP.

"Well, she has in this portrait you took of her," replied Roderick.

"And this portrait of Mr Owl shows him with rabbit's legs," pointed out Hammy, as the next print was finished.

Poor Guinea Pig was speechless. Every print he made had the wrong head on the wrong legs.

"It's as though all the negatives had been broken and put together again with the wrong pieces," he said. And then, after a moment's thought, "Perhaps I *have* got ghosts after all…!"

"No," said Roderick, with a tear in his eye. "You haven't got ghosts…It was me." And he went on to tell how he had dropped the negatives and glued them all together again.

"Oh, never mind," said GP. "I think I was fed up with photography,

anyway…The lights are too bright, and much too hot."

And then, as if to change the subject, Hammy said, "Oh, you are a clever Guinea Pig - look, this picture you took of Roderick and me is fine. We've both got the correct legs on."

And, of course, they had.